Disney Vampirina

VEE'S FIRST DAY OF SCHOOL

Adapted by Chelsea Beyl

Based on the episode "Portrait of a Vampire" by Chelsea Beyl

Illustrated by the Imaginism Studio and the Disney Storybook Art Team

A GOLDEN BOOK • NEW YORK

rhcbooks.com
ISBN 978-0-7364-3843-8
Printed in the United States of America
10 9 8 7 6 5 4 3 2 1

Tomorrow is a big day for Vampirina. It's her very first day of human school in Pennsylvania.

"I've got my lucky troll pen, my history book, and my monster ruler!" Vee says to her friend Poppy. "I can't wait! I loved school back in TRANSYLVANIA."

But back in **TRANSYLVANIA**, school was a little bit different.

Vee used to play her **SPOOKYLELE** in music class.

She studied **HAUNTED HISTORY** and **MONSTER MATH**.

She even made **MAGIC POTIONS** in science class!

Poppy giggles. "School in Pennsylvania isn't quite like that.
We'll play kazoos in music class, you'll read books that won't
fly away, and you'll get your picture taken for the class tree,"
she explains.

"Wow! We didn't have a class tree in Transylvania," says Vee,
feeling excited.

The next day, it's time for Vee to go to school.

"Uppity-up! Wake up, screamyhead!" says Demi
as he flies into Vampirina's room.

"It's my first day of school!" shouts Vee. She zooms
to the closet and gets dressed super quick.

"Adorable!" says Demi. "That's the perfect first-day-
of-human-school outfit."

Downstairs, Vee's mom and dad wish her luck.

"Here's your favorite lunch, batkins. It's black jumping beans with my SPOOKY sauce!" says Oxana.

"And here's a gift for your teacher," says Boris. He hands Vee a special plant.

"One more thing," says Oxana. "A *ghoul*-luck kiss!" Vee's family kisses her good-bye.

Vampirina meets her friends Poppy, Bridget, and Edgar at school.

"Hi, Vee!" says Poppy.

"Ready for your first day?" asks Bridget.

Vee looks up at her new school and gulps. "I feel like I have
SPIDERS in my stomach," says Vee. She's nervous!

"Don't worry," says Poppy. "You'll be great . . . and we'll be right
here with you!"

When Vee enters her new classroom, she sees
a colorful tree on the wall.

"This is the class tree I told you about!" says Poppy.
"You'll get your picture taken and add your leaf today."

Vee can't wait!

Vee meets her teacher and gives him the plant. "This is for you, Mr. Gore!" says Vee. "It's from my mom's garden."

But when Mr. Gore takes the plant, it chomps at him. "Ahhh! Chompy!" he says, a little spooked.

"Sorry!" says Vee. "Plants from Transylvania get pretty hungry."

Mr. Gore asks Vee to introduce herself to the class.
Vee is so excited to say hi to everyone, she zooms to
the front of the room with vampire speed.

WHOOSH!

Papers fly everywhere, and Mr. Gore almost falls over!
"Whoa! Speedy!" he says.

"Oops! Sorry . . . again!" says Vee. She remembers that
she can't use her vampire powers at human school.

"Hi, I'm Vampirina. From Transylvania!" she says. "You can call me Vee."

Suddenly, everyone hears a pop!

POP! POP! POPPITY-POP!

Vee's lunch box is hopping up and down. Now the whole class is spooked!

"Ahhh!" the kids shout.

"Oh, no!" says Vee. "Sorry! Must be those jumping beans my mom packed for lunch." She hides her lunch box, feeling a little embarrassed. Her first day of school isn't going so well.

Vee's friends tell her not to worry. "Art class will help you feel better," says Poppy. "We're making paintings."

Mr. Gore hands out trays of colorful paints.

"The assignment is to paint something that is special to you," he says.

As Vee's friends get started on their paintings,
Mr. Gore tells Vee that it's time to take her picture
for the class tree. "As soon as your leaf is on the tree,
you'll be an official member of our class," he says.
Vee is thrilled!

"Smile!" says Mr. Gore. But when he takes
Vee's picture—FLASH!—the bright light
startles her and . . .

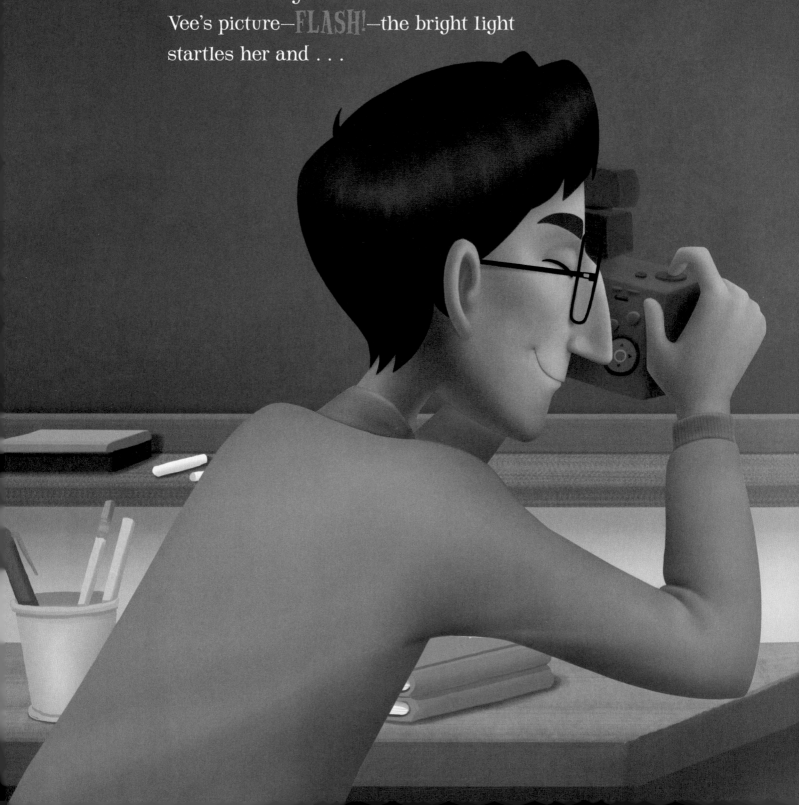

. . . she turns into a bat! **POOF!**

"Oh, no!" cries Vee when she sees
the picture. She can't be a bat for the
class tree! Vee's first day of human school
is officially a disaster.

When Vee arrives home, her family asks how her first day went.

"It was like a sunny day in Transylvania," she says. "Terrible!" She shows her family her bat picture for the class tree. "I got a case of the BATTYS!"

"Don't worry, little Vee," says Boris. "Bright lights startle
lots of vampires. Even Uncle Dieter."

Vee's parents explain that Uncle Dieter turns into a bat every
time a camera flashes.

"That's why vampires have their portraits painted," says Oxana.

But Vee is still disappointed. "Everybody has their picture on the class tree," she says. "If I can't take a picture, I'll never be a real part of the class."

Vampirina thinks maybe she shouldn't even go to school at all.

Poppy looks at the painting of Uncle Dieter and gets
an idea. "Leave it to me!" she says.

The next day, Vampirina returns to school. She walks into the classroom and sees the class tree. Vee feels sad that she doesn't have a picture to put on it.

But Poppy has a surprise. "I didn't know what to do for my art project, but I got the perfect idea when I was at your house yesterday," she tells Vee.

Poppy holds up her painting.
It's a portrait of Vampirina!
"I painted a portrait of my new
best friend," she says. "Because
you're special to me!"

"I love it!" says Vee. "It's my favorite picture of myself ever! You really brought out the blue in my cheeks."

Vee asks Mr. Gore if she can use Poppy's painting for the class tree. Mr. Gore says it's a great idea, so Vee adds her leaf.

Vee thanks Poppy and gives her a big hug. "I think school in Pennsylvania is going to be just fine."